characters created by
lauren child

HELP!

I really

mean it!

PUFFIN

Text based on the script

written by Anna Starkey

Illustrations from the TV animation

produced by Tiger Aspect

PUFFIN BOOKS
Published by the Penguin Group: London, New York, Australia,
Canada, India, Ireland, New Zealand and South Africa
Penguin Books Ltd, Registered Offices: 80 Strand, London WC2R 0RL, England

puffinbooks.com

This edition published in Great Britain in Puffin Books 2012
001 – 10 9 8 7 6 5 4 3 2 1
Text and illustrations copyright © Lauren Child/Tiger Aspect Productions Limited, 2008
Charlie and Lola word and logo ® and © Lauren Child, 2005
Charlie and Lola is produced by Tiger Aspect Productions
All rights reserved
The moral right of the author/illustrator has been asserted
Manufactured in China
ISBN: 978-0-718-19528-1
This edition produced for the Book People Ltd,
Hall Wood Avenue, Haydock, St Helens, WA11 9UL

I have this little sister Lola.
          She is small and very funny.
Today we are looking after Caspar,
          Granny and Grandpa's cat.
Lola REALLY loves Caspar.

Lola says,
    "Look, Charlie! Caspar is playing
a game with us."

So I say, "Caspar is a cat.
        He might not like all of your games."

"He definitely likes this one," says Lola.

Then Lola says,
        "Lotta, did you know that
Caspar is an actual tiger..."

"Oooh! Lola, what are those noises?"
asks Lotta.

Lola says,
"I don't know. But it's all right
because we are with Caspar.

Oh... where's Caspar gone?"

And Lotta says,
    "Oh! Yes! Where's Caspar gone?"

Then Lola and Lotta shout,
    "HEEEELLLLPPPPP!"

Me and Marv run in and ask,
"Are you all right?!"

And Lola says,
"Yes, Charlie! Caspar was just going to
rescue me and Lotta from some tigers."

So I say,
"Lola, you must ONLY call for help
          if you REALLY mean it."

And Lola says,
"Sorry, Charlie. We only said HELP by accident."

Lotta says,
"It was very **funny** when we said HELP
and Charlie and Marv
came running in."

And Lola asks,
        "Do you think if we say **help** now,
        they will come in again?"

"HELP! HELP! HELP! HELP!"

"What's the matter?!"
                me and Marv ask.

And Lola says, "Nothing, Charlie..."

        So I say, "Oh. I get it. Very funny."

"We won't do it again," says Lola.

So I ask, "Do you promise?"

And Lola says,
        "We absolutely do **promise**."

Later, Lotta says,
  "Look! Caspar likes **dressing up**.

Do you think **cats** like wearing **hats**?"

  "Oh! I know they do," says Lola.

"And they like going for
carriage rides, too.

Come on, Caspar.
It's time for a **ride**."

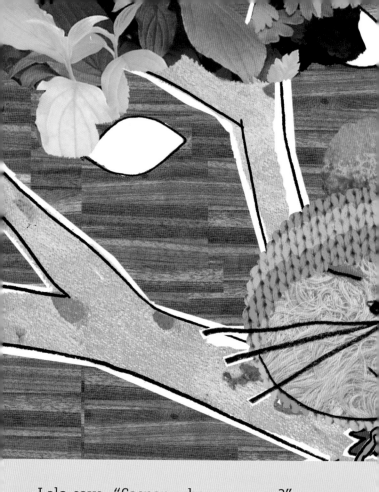

Lola says, "Caspar, where are you?"

"Are you here, Caspar?" says Lotta

"Caspar! Where are you?"

Then Lola and Lotta look out of the window.

"Oh no! HELP, Charlie! HELP!"

"Caspar!

CASPAR!"

And I ask, "What is it this time, Lola?"

Lola says,
        "Caspar's stuck right up in the
sky, and he's crying and his
                hat's gone all ᴡoᴎᴋy!"

So I say,
      "Sorry, Lola. It's not going to
work this time."

      And Lola says, "But Charlie,
we really, REALLY need you to h**e**l**p**..."

"Charlie and Marv don't believe me
so we've got to get Caspar down by ourselves.
Please come down, Caspar!"

And Lotta says, "PLEASE!"

Then Caspar climbs
    higher up the tree.

And Lola shouts,
    "Noooooo! Charlie! HELP!"

Me and Marv run over and Lola says,
            "See? I did **really** need you."

    And I say, "But I didn't believe you
                because you kept **shouting** HELP
when you didn't mean it."

Lola and Lotta say,
            "Sorry, Charlie. Sorry, Marv."

And I say,
            "Look! Caspar has **jumped**
      on to Marv's balcony!"

Then Marv says, "Err... Charlie,
why is that **cat** wearing a **hat**?"

So I say, "**Cats** don't like **hats**, Lola."

And Marv says, "I would run away,
too, if I had to wear a **hat** like that!"